# Eoin McLaughlin ★ Polly Dunbar

# The Roar

There were so many things that
Tortoise wanted to do.
So many games to play and
rocks to climb and . . .

... Oops!

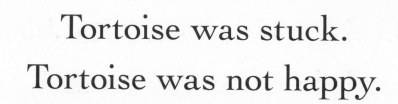

Tortoise was stuck.
Tortoise was not happy.

"I'm NOT HAPPY," said Tortoise.

"You should dig a hole," said Rabbit.
"That's what I do when I'm cross."

"I'm too cross for digging.
And much too upside down."

"Cheer up!" said Fox.
"I've brought you this
smelly, old boot."

"I'm much too upset for smelly boots!"

"How about a hug?" said Hedgehog.

Tortoise was angry.
Even a hug could not help.

"Well, to cheer someone up,
you must try to understand what
they're feeling," said Owl.

Hedgehog tried to
feel like Tortoise.

It was hard.

After all, Hedgehog was
a hedgehog.

But Hedgehog
kept on trying.

Until,

eventually . . .

"I'd be angry if I was stuck," said Hedgehog.

"I fell," said Tortoise.

"And I don't like it. And I'm not happy ...
and that's what it is."

Hedgehog listened.

And the more Hedgehog listened,

the more Tortoise spoke.

Then they fell quiet

and watched the clouds together,

until –

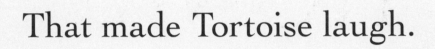

That made Tortoise laugh.

"Would you mind?" said Tortoise.
"Oh, of course," said Hedgehog.

"If I ever get stuck again . . .

…then I hope I get stuck with you!"

There were so many things that
Tortoise and Hedgehog wanted to do.
So many games to play and
rocks to climb and …

...Oops!

For anyone who sometimes roars.
And everyone who always listens.

(And James, who always helps when we get stuck.)
P.D. and E.M.

Faber has published children's books since 1929.
T. S. Eliot's *Old Possum's Book of Practical Cats*
and Ted Hughes' *The Iron Man* were amongst
the first. Our catalogue at the time said that
'it is by reading such books that children learn
the difference between the shoddy and the
genuine'. We still believe in the power of reading
to transform children's lives. All our books are
chosen with the express intention of growing
a love of reading, a thirst for knowledge and
to cultivate empathy. We pride ourselves on
responsible editing. Last but not least, we believe
in kind and inclusive books in which all children
feel represented and important.

First published in the UK in 2022
First published in the US in 2022
by Faber and Faber Limited
Bloomsbury House, 74–77 Great Russell Street, London WC1B 3DA
Text © Eoin McLaughlin, 2022  Illustrations © Polly Dunbar, 2022
Designed by Faber and Faber
HB ISBN 978–0–571–37434–2
PB ISBN 978–0–571–37436–6
All rights reserved.
Printed in India
2 4 6 8 10 9 7 5 3 1
The moral rights of Eoin McLaughlin and Polly Dunbar have been asserted.
A CIP record for this book is available from the British Library.